Immortals
H

MAC

LONDON·SYDNEY

Franklin Watts
First published in Great Britain in 2016 by The Watts Publishing Group

PB ISBN 978 1 4451 5102 1
ebook ISBN 978 1 4451 5124 3
Library ebook ISBN 978 1 4451 5123 6

1 3 5 7 9 10 8 6 4 2

Printed and bound by CPI Group (UK) Ltd, Croydon, CR0 4YY

Franklin Watts
An imprint of
Hachette Children's Group
Part of The Watts Publishing Group
Carmelite House
50 Victoria Embankment
London EC4Y 0DZ

An Hachette UK Company
www.hachette.co.uk

www.franklinwatts.co.uk

How to be a hero

This book is not like others you have read. This is a choose-your-own-destiny book where YOU are the hero of the adventure.

Each section of this book is numbered. At the end of most sections, you will have to make a choice. Each choice will take you to a different section of the book.

If you choose correctly, you will succeed. But be careful. If you make a bad choice, you may have to start the adventure again. If this happens, make sure you learn from your mistake!

Go to the next page to start your adventure. And remember, don't be a zero, be a hero!

You are an agent of the Global Intelligence Agency (GIA). Your code name is Agent Scorpio.

You have succeeded in many dangerous missions. Your latest triumph has been to break into the headquarters of the Purple Dragon Triad in Hong King and upload all the details of their crooked deals to the GIA. But the Triad bosses have discovered this, and you are now in deep water.

Go to 1.

1

You guide your speedboat across the crowded water of Hong Kong's Victoria Harbour, jinking around ferries and barges. Behind you, a boat of Triad gangsters is in hot pursuit. The thugs yell threats and fire at you with machine guns. They seem annoyed.

Another boat appears to your left, forcing you into a dead end.

If you want to call for backup, go to 14.
If you would rather use your own skills to get out of trouble, go to 27.

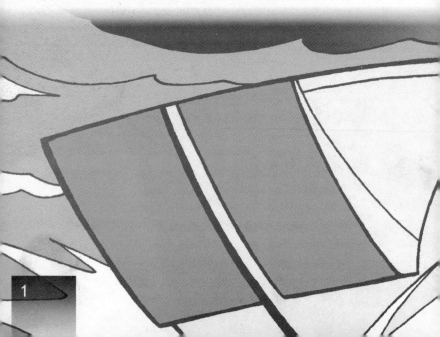

2

You select flight mode. The butterfly-wing doors fold out and the concealed jet engines roar.

You take off and make a steep turn, diving on your attackers. You pop up and fire your concealed autocannons. The SUV explodes. The fireball hits your car.

Alarms shriek. Your engines cut out. You struggle for control, but it's no good. You are about to crash! You press the PANIC button.

Go to 49.

3

You approach the doors to the Mammon building. They slide open.

A uniformed guard at the reception desk glares at you. "We're closed."

You smile. "I visited Mr Mammon earlier today. I think I left my briefcase in his office."

"Top floor." The guard points to an

executive lift. You walk over and push a button to call the lift. It descends and the doors open.

Two more guards step out, guns at the ready. You duck and roll for cover as they open fire.

If you chose the explosive watch and want to use it, go to 42.

If you chose the other watch, use the PANIC button and go to 49.

4

"Fly lower," you tell the pilot.

The plane drops into the seething clouds. Instantly, it is buffeted by the storm. The engines falter.

"It's too dangerous to jump," reports the pilot.

If you want to order the pilot to fly higher, go to 30.

If you want to ignore the pilot's advice and jump, go to 17.

5

You activate your watch. The electromagnetic pulse fries the electronic circuits of the drones, which drop out of the sky. Luckily, bushes break your fall.

You head back to Mammon's dome

and use your unarmed combat skills to overcome the guards. You enter the base and find yourself in a corridor with a sign pointing left to the radio room, and another pointing right to the satellite control room.

If you want to head for the radio room, go to 44.

If you want to follow the sign to satellite control, go to 13.

6

Mr Melville meets you in the ops room. "Agent Scorpio," he says. "You have a new mission." He presses a button and a holographic image of three satellites appears.

"These are experimental military satellites," Melville explains, "equipped with laser weapons. They were developed for use against Near Earth Objects — to help prevent an asteroid colliding with Earth. The trouble is someone else has taken control of them."

A new image appears — a fairground laughing clown.

Between peals of insane laughter, a mechanical voice says, "These satellites will destroy every major city on Earth, unless all governments agree to my demands."

You scratch your head. "It looks like this joker wants to take over the world!"

"Agreed," says Melville. "Your job is to stop him. I'd like to introduce you to our new weapons expert."

If you want to see the weapons expert, go to 45.

If you want to get on with the mission, go to 23.

7

As you head towards the southbound tunnel, the SUV is close behind you.

You brake behind a big, slow lorry. Your pursuers catch up, still firing. You pull out to overtake, straight into the path of a fire engine coming the other way! You're going to crash! You press the PANIC button.

Go to 49.

8

You dive into the chute and slide straight down. You land in the basement next to a fire escape door. You get out of the building and run as fast as you can.

The Mammon building explodes behind you, throwing you to the ground. You sit up, dazed, as pieces of glass and metal shower down around you. There is a ringing in your ears. You realise it is your watch phone.

The call is from Melanie Goodness. "Sebastian Mammon's private jet just took off. He's heading for an island he owns in

the South Pacific. We've received word that an air strike has been ordered to destroy the island!"

"I need to get to that island to make sure Mammon can't escape and use the satellites. Call the Air Force — I need a lift. And pack me my jet suit. Please."

Go to 12.

You dive towards the sea and speed over the waves. The missiles are gaining on you. A cliff looms ahead. You spot a narrow passage in the cliff wall and fly through it. The Warbird missiles smash into the cliff and explode behind you.

You cut your engines and use your parachute to land. You shrug off the jetpack. You are about to report your safe arrival when a mechanical hum arises all round you and photo-electric eyes blink open. You are surrounded by spy-drones!

If you want to fight the spy-drones, go to 21.

If you decide to allow them to capture you, go to 47.

10

The watches sound useful. "Why can't I take both?"

"Who wears two watches?"

"Good point."

If you want to take the electromagnetic watch, go to 19.

If you decide to take the explosive magnetic mine watch, go to 32.

11

You hover over the car, looking for survivors.

Suddenly, your vehicle judders as bullets slam into it. The helicopter is attacking you! You try to escape but your steering is damaged. Alarms sound as the engines fail. You are out of altitude and out of options.

You press the PANIC button.

Go to 49.

12

A few hours later you are over the Pacific in the bomb bay of a B-2 Stealth Bomber. You are wearing a jet suit, preparing to jump.

The pilot's voice comes over the intercom. "There's bad weather around the island. Do you want to climb above it, or go in under it?"

If you want to climb, go to 30.
If you want to go in low, go to 4.

13

You find the satellite controls and try to disarm them; but you are locked out.

Mammon's face appears on a screen.

"Sorry, Agent Scorpio. I control the satellites from my space-plane. My associates and I are about to leave the island in case your organisation orders an air strike. We are heading to our secret moon base while the Earth descends into chaos. Goodbye!"

If you want to get off the island before the air strike, go to 38.

If you want to find the Warbird missile controls, go to 35.

14

You call GIA HQ, and quickly explain your situation. "A little help would be welcome."

"It's on its way," the operator tells you.

A Eurocopter buzzes overhead and descends rapidly. As it hovers over your boat, you reach up and grab a landing skid. The helicopter lifts away. The pursuing gangsters fire up at you, but you are soon out of range.

Your watch phone rings. One handed, you answer it.

"Agent Scorpio." It's your boss, Mr Melville. "Are you busy at the moment?"

"No," you say, "just hanging around."

"Then come in. I have a job for you."

Go to 40.

15

You pull ahead of the SUV, but you can't shake it off.

You call GIA HQ on your watch phone. Doctor Goodness answers. "How's the car?"

Another burst of gunfire rakes across the bodywork. "Bulletproof, I hope," you say. You tell her about your pursuer. "I want to know about any mobile phone calls coming from that car."

"I'm on it," Doctor Goodness replies.

You come to a junction. One road goes to Tower Bridge, the other to the Blackwall Tunnel.

If you want to head towards Tower Bridge, go to 28.

To choose the Blackwall Tunnel road, go to 7.

16

You fly to the tower block where Mammon Industries has its offices. A few lights are on, but all seems quiet. You land in a nearby street.

If you want to use the front door to enter the building, go to 3.

If you would rather try to find a way to sneak in, go to 29.

17

You open the bomb bay doors and trigger the release clips.

You drop into the boiling clouds as your jet engines ignite, speeding you through the air. Lightning flashes around you. You are thrown about by the strong wind. Your visor is streaked with rain.

At last, you drop into the clear air below the clouds. But your relief is short lived. Your suit's tracking systems reports a weapon lock-on, and that Warbird missiles have been fired to intercept you!

If you want to try to outdistance the missiles, go to 22.

If you want to climb and lose the missiles in the storm, go to 43.

If you want to go low and try to out-manoeuvre the missiles, go to 9.

18

You reach for your magnetic mine watch. You can use it to destroy the drone that is carrying you.

Then you remember that you have already used your watch. There is no escape.

You press the PANIC button.

Go to 49.

19

"I'll take the electromagnetic pulse watch," you say.

"Remember," says Doctor Goodness, "you can only use that watch to knock out a computer system or electronics."

To change your mind, go to 32.
To stick with your choice, go to 36.

20

You press the button to call the lift. It makes a loud beep noise, and the guard on the desk spots you. He activates an alarm and two guards dash from a side room.

If you chose the explosive watch, go to 42.

If you chose the other watch, use the PANIC button and go to 49.

21

You take out your laser pen to fire at the drones. But there are too many and they are too fast. They return fire with plasma bolts. Soon you are numb with the shock of these miniature lightning strikes and your pen needs recharging.

To use your PANIC button, go to 49.

To surrender to the drones, go to 47.

22

You turn the suit's engines to maximum speed.

It is no use. The missiles are far faster. They are still gaining on you.

If you want to climb and lose the missiles in the storm, go to 43.

If you want to go low and try to out-manoeuvre the missiles, go to 9.

23

You scowl. "For once can I just get on with the mission?"

Mr Melville shrugs. "Well, I really think—"

"I don't know why these useless geeks think they are so special..." you say, heading for the door.

You bump into another gorilla. It attacks you with a perfect judo throw, then hurls a banana at you. The yellow missile spins around you trailing a thin, unbreakable cord. Soon you are trussed like a chicken.

The gorilla takes its head off. The woman inside the gorilla suit gives you a friendly grin. "Hello. I'm the new 'useless geek'. I really think you need to see my lab."

You pull a face. "I'm a little tied up at the moment..."

You wait while the woman unties you.

Go to 45.

24

You approach the helicopter. Without warning, it turns to attack you, but fires

wide as you take avoiding action.

Doctor Goodness calls as you twist the wheel to avoid another burst of gunfire. "This had better be good news..." you say.

"The driver of the car following you made a call to Mammon Industries."

"What a bad man!" you say. "Trying to kill me AND using a mobile phone while driving."

You think hard. Sebastian Mammon is big in the telecommunications industry — could he have taken over the satellites?

You pop up the car's concealed autocannons and fire at the helicopter. It crashes into the river. Circling overhead, you see the River Police picking up survivors.

To report in to GIA HQ, go to 37.

If you want to head for Mammon Industries HQ, go to 16.

25

You head down the stairs, but before you reach the third floor, there is a tremendous explosion. You are choked by dust as the building collapses around you. The stairs tilt, glass and girders rain down as you press the PANIC button.

Go to 49.

26

You find signs for the hangar, and follow them.

You arrive just as the space-plane is taxiing for take-off. As it gathers speed, you race towards it and manage to jump onto the landing gear. The plane takes off, and you realise it is impossible to maintain your hold. As the wheels retract, you lose your grip and fall. In despair, you press the PANIC button.

Go to 49.

27

You spin the wheel to head back between the oncoming Triad launches. They change course to intercept you.

At the last moment, you send the engine

into reverse. Your boat comes to a dead stop. The gangsters scream as their boats collide, hurling them into the water.

As you turn and speed away, your watch phone rings. You answer it.

It is your boss, Mr Melville. "Agent Scorpio, do you have plans for the rest of the day?"

"No," you say, "frankly, I'm all at sea."

"Then come in. I have a job for you."

Go to 40.

28

You head for Tower Bridge, but as you approach it, lights flash and the barriers come down. The bridge is opening to allow a boat to pass underneath!

If you want to jump the bridge, go to 33.

If you decide to stop, go to 46.

29

You find a delivery door at the back of the building and use your laser pen to cut around the lock. You sneak through storage rooms until you come to a door with a glass panel. You can see a guard at a desk in the reception area. He has his back to you! Carefully, you creep past to the lift and stairs. A board shows that Sebastian Mammon's office is on the top floor.

If you want to head up the stairs, go to 34.

If you decide to press the button to use the lift, go to 20.

30

"Fly higher," you tell the pilot.

The engines roar as the plane climbs —
but within moments you hear the pilot say,
"They have missile lock-on!" There is an
explosion and the fuselage fills with smoke
"Bail out!" orders the pilot.

To use your PANIC button, go to 49.
If you want to use your jet suit, go to 17.

31

You activate the magnetic mine watch and
attach it to the cargo drone. The watch
explodes, destroying the drone. It drops
you, but you are dazed by the blast and
stunned by your fall. You can only watch
as the other drones close in. You press the
PANIC button.

Go to 49.

32

"I'll take the magnetic mine watch," you
say.

"Remember," says Doctor Goodness, "that watch will only destroy whatever it is in direct contact with."

If you decide to change your mind, go to 19.

If you want to stick with your choice, go to 36.

33

You floor the accelerator and smash through the barriers.

As you hit the moving ramp of the bridge, you select flight mode. The butterfly-wing doors deploy and jet engines roar as you take off. In your mirrors you see your pursuers' car topple over the end of the ramp and plunge into the River Thames.

A helicopter appears and hovers over the water where the car is sinking fast.

If you want to help the helicopter search for survivors, go to 11.

If you want to take a good look at the helicopter, go to 24.

34

Slightly breathless from your climb, you find Mammon's office.

The office is empty. All the cabinets have been cleared and only dangling cables show where the computers have been.

You lean back against Mammon's desk to think — and your bottom pushes a penholder, which clicks downwards. A wall panel slides open to reveal a steel-lined escape chute. The room lights flash red. A recorded voice announces, "Building auto-destruct activated: ninety seconds to detonation."

Uh-oh, you think. You have set off a booby trap!

To use Mammon's escape chute, go to 8.
If you want to use the stairs, go to 25.

35

You find the Warbird controls. You lock the targeting system onto Mammon's space-plane and fire missiles!

You wait anxiously. To your relief, the computer reports a hit! You check the instrument panel, and see that Mammon's plane must be damaged. It is going down!

If you want to go to the radio room to report to the GIA, go to 39.

If you want to try to destroy the satellites, go to 48.

36

Doctor Goodness leads you through a door into a garage. Lights come on to reveal a McLaren 650S supercar. You whistle. "Nice car!"

"It flies." Melanie Goodness hands you the key ring. "Your PANIC button also locks and unlocks the car. Don't get the buttons mixed up, Agent Scorpio."

"Hmmm — I saw the prototype of this. Didn't it crash?"

"Yes, but we know what went wrong. I'm almost sure."

You shrug, get into the car and start the engine. As you close the doors, she calls, "Try not to break it, Agent Scorpio!"

Go to 41.

37

You return to GIA Headquarters and enter the control room.

Mr Melville glares at you. "Why are you here?"

"To find out more details about the call from the car, and discuss..."

Mr Melville is furious. "There are no more details! There's nothing to discuss! Get over to Mammon's offices at once — it may already be too late!"

Go to 16.

38

You follow signs for the landing stage and find yourself in a small harbour with cliffs on three sides. Tied up to the tiny dock is a powerful motorboat. You untie it, power up the outboard engine and head for the open sea.

Before you get far, the sky lights up with a huge explosion. The air strike has started! Boulders fall from the cliffs, blocking the harbour mouth and trapping you inside. More explosions follow and the whole cliff falls towards you! You hit the PANIC button.

Go to 49.

39

You find the radio room. "Call off the air strike! Mammon's plane is going down."

"We can see that for ourselves!" Mr Melville's voice crackles over the radio. "What are you waiting for? Can you stop the satellites?"

You press the radio's transmit button. "I can try."

Go to 48.

40

You fly back to London and take a taxi to the zoo. You head for the Gorilla Kingdom.

You slip round the back of the building. A retina scan allows you through a hidden door. As it opens, you find yourself facing a powerful male silverback gorilla!

"Afternoon, Rodney," you say. "On guard duty again?"

"Yes, worse luck," says the man in the gorilla suit. He moves away from the doorway. "Go through. Mr Melville is expecting you."

Soon you are in a lift, going down to the secret GIA base beneath the zoo.

Go to 6.

You drive up a ramp, and a concealed exit lets you out into Regent's Park.

You decide to see if a contact at the American Embassy knows anything about the missing satellites. But as you head towards the embassy, a black SUV pulls alongside you. An Uzi MP2 machine gun is thrust out of the side window and opens fire!

If you want to switch to flight mode, go to 2.

If you want to pull ahead and see what your attackers do, go to 15.

42

As the man from the desk runs to help the
the guards, you take off your watch and
attach it to a cleaning trolley standing
by the lift. You push this towards your
attackers and dive behind a pillar.

The trolley explodes sending mops,
brooms and buckets flying. The guards are
stunned.

"That's what I call a clean sweep," you
mutter as you step over them. You head
for the stairs in case there are more guards
coming down in the lift.

Go to 34.

43

You climb into the clouds. Once again you
are hurled around by the storm. Your suit's
tracking system fails: you can only hope
that the Warbird missiles' guidance systems
have also been damaged!

Half-blinded by lightning, you drop out of
the clouds again — only to realise that the

missiles have been tracking you. They are
right behind you!

**If you want to use your PANIC button,
go to 49.**

**If you want to fly as low as you can, go
to 9.**

44

You use the radio to call the GIA emergency
frequency. "Mammon is here. He has
control of the satellites!" you report.

The reply comes, not from the GIA
operator, but from Mammon himself. "My
associates and I are about to leave the
island in my space-plane, heading to our
secret moon base while the Earth descends
into chaos... Goodbye, Agent Scorpio!"

Time is running out! Mammon will escape
from the island before the air strike!

**If you want to try to stop the space-
plane taking off, go to 26.**

**If you want to find the Warbird missile
controls, go to 35.**

45

You are led into a well-equipped lab.

"My name is Doctor Goodness." Mr Melville's weapons expert shakes your hand. "Melanie Goodness. Now, pay attention, Agent Scorpio." She hands you a key ring.

"This is our latest gadget. A PANIC button. It stands for Personal Automatic Need-Induced reCovery. It's an experimental teleport device. If you are faced with great danger, press the button. It will bring you back here, to this moment in time. Roughly."

"Er... Right." You pick up an ordinary-looking ballpoint. "Laser pen?"

"Yes, take that. And one of these." She holds up two watches. "This one delivers an electromagnetic pulse that will fry any electronic circuits within a ten metre radius. And this one is a high-explosive magnetic mine."

To try to take both watches, go to 10.

If you want to take the electromagnetic watch, go to 19.

If you decide to take the explosive magnetic mine watch, go to 32.

46

You slam on the brakes and screech to a halt. Your pursuers are right behind you. The SUV smashes into the rear of your car, forcing it over the edge of the bridge. It plunges into the water.

"It's a shame this model doesn't drive underwater," you say. There is nothing for it. You hit the PANIC button.

Go to 49.

47

You raise your hands. The drones hustle you down a narrow track to a domed building.

Inside the dome, human guards take you to Sebastian Mammon.

"Agent Scorpio," he sneers. "You are too late. The deadline for world governments to surrender has passed! The countdown has begun. London, New York, Moscow, Beijing — all will be destroyed." He gives an evil chuckle. "In the meantime, there is an active volcano at the heart of this island.

My drones will take you to inspect it —
very closely!"

Minutes later, you are being carried up
the slopes of the volcano by a large cargo
drone escorted by a dozen spy drones.

If you are wearing the electromagnetic watch, go to 5.

If you are still wearing the magnetic mine watch, go to 31.

If you used the magnetic mine watch at the Mammon building, go to 18.

48

With the destruction of Mammon's space-plane, you find that the satellite control board is now active. You command the satellites to self-destruct.

The satellites on the display wink out of existence one by one, and you breathe a sigh of relief — but then the ground shakes, throwing you off your feet. You think it's the air strike, but then a recorded voice announces, "Auto-destruct activated. Volcanic eruption in progress."

"Oh, no," you groan, "not again!"

The dome collapses around you and molten lava from the volcano flows in. You reach for the PANIC button but as another shockwave hits, you drop it and it rolls through a crack in the floor and into a lava stream!

The volcano explodes. As the island sinks into the sea, you dive from a collapsing cliff and swim for your life.

The sea bubbles around you, and you think about the spicy curry you had for dinner last night. You give a relieved sigh as a miniature submarine surfaces just ahead. A hatch opens and Melanie Goodness pops her head out. She grins. "Hello. Would you like to be rescued?"

Go to 50.

49

You find yourself back in Doctor Goodness's lab.

She scowls as you fully rematerialise. "I thought you were the best, Agent Scorpio."

"I am the best!" you tell her.

"Then prove it! Start making smart decisions." She hands you another key ring. "And try not to mess up this time."

Go to 41.

A short while later, you are standing on the flight deck of an aircraft carrier.

You thank Doctor Goodness for her timely rescue. "All part of the service," she smiles.

You watch as Mammon and his supporters are fished out of the wreck of their space-plane.

Mr Melville joins you. "The owners of the satellites aren't too happy that you destroyed them," he says. "They wanted them back." He smiles. "But the GIA approves your action. You are a hero!"

Immortals

HERO

I HERO Quiz

Test yourself with this special quiz. It has been designed to see how much you remember about the book you've just read. Can you get all five answers right?

To download the answer sheets simply visit:

www.hachettechildrens.co.uk

Enter the "Teacher Zone" and search "Immortals".

Question 1

Which of these gadgets is not offered to you by Doctor Goodness?

A   explosive mine watch

B   laser pen

C   spy drone

D   electromagnetic watch

Question 2

What are you forced to jump down to escape from the Mammon building?

A   a ladder

B   a lift shaft

C   a ramp

D   a metal chute

Question 3

How do you shoot down Mammon's space-plane?

A   with missiles

B   with a laser satellite

C   with the explosive mine watch

D   with your car's autocannons

Question 4

Which zoo is GIA HQ hidden underneath?

A   New York City

B   San Diego

C   London

D   Beijing

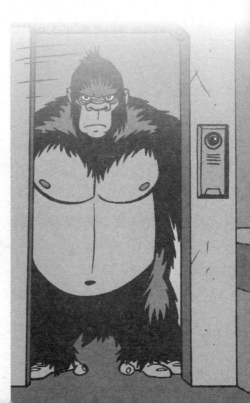

Question 5

What is the name of your boss at GIA?

A   Dr Goodness

B   Mr Melville

C   Dr Melanie

D   Mr Mammon

About the 2Steves

"The 2Steves" are Britain's most popular writing double act for young people, specialising in comedy and adventure. They perform regularly in schools and libraries, and at festivals, taking the power of words and story to audiences of all ages.

Together they have written many books, including the *Crime Team* series. Find out what they've been up to at: **www.the2steves.net**

About the illustrator: Jack Lawrence

Jack Lawrence is a successful freelance comics illustrator, working on titles such as *A.T.O.M.*, Cartoon Network, *Doctor Who Adventures*, *2000 AD*, *Transformers* and *Spider-Man Tower of Power*. He also works as a freelance toy designer.

Jack lives in Maidstone in Kent with his partner and two cats.

Have you completed the I HERO Quests?

Battle with aliens in Tyranno Quest:

AIR BLAST
Steve Barlow - Steve Skidmore

978 1 4451 0875 9 pb
978 1 4451 1345 6 ebook

FIRE STORM
Steve Barlow - Steve Skidmore

978 1 4451 0876 6 pb
978 1 4451 1346 3 ebook

ICE STRIKE
Steve Barlow - Steve Skidmore

978 1 4451 0877 3 pb
978 1 4451 1347 0 ebook

EARTH ATTACK
Steve Barlow - Steve Skidmore

978 1 4451 0878 0 pb
978 1 4451 1348 7 ebook

Defeat the Red Queen in Blood Crown Quest:

SANDS OF BLOOD
Steve Barlow - Steve Skidmore

978 1 4451 1499 6 pb
978 1 4451 1503 0 ebook

DRAGON MOUNTAIN
Steve Barlow - Steve Skidmore

978 1 4451 1500 9 pb
978 1 4451 1504 7 ebook

DEMON SEA
Steve Barlow - Steve Skidmore

978 1 4451 1501 6 pb
978 1 4451 1505 4 ebook

CITY OF THE DEAD
Steve Barlow - Steve Skidmore

978 1 4451 1502 3 pb
978 1 4451 1506 1 ebook

Save planet Earth in Atlantis Quest:

MENACE FROM THE DEEP
Steve Barlow - Steve Skidmore

978 1 4451 2867 2 pb
978 1 4451 2868 9 ebook

OCEAN ALLIANCE
Steve Barlow - Steve Skidmore

978 1 4451 2870 2 pb
978 1 4451 2871 9 ebook

BATTLE FOR THE SEAS
Steve Barlow - Steve Skidmore

978 1 4451 2876 4 pb
978 1 4451 2877 1 ebook

ATLANTIS ASSAULT
Steve Barlow - Steve Skidmore

978 1 4451 2873 3 pb
978 1 4451 2874 0 ebook

More I HERO Immortals

978 1 4451 4081 0 pb
978 1 4451 4082 7 eBook

You are the last Dragon Warrior.
A dark, evil force stirs within the
Iron Mines. Grull the Cruel's
army is on the march! YOU must
stop Grull.

978 1 4451 4088 9 pb
978 1 4451 4087 2 eBook

You are a noble mermaid —
your father is King Edmar.
The Tritons are attacking your home
of Coral City. YOU must save the Merrow
people by finding the Lady of the Sea.

978 1 4451 4084 1 pb
978 1 4451 4085 8 eBook

You are Olympian, a superhero.
Your enemy, Doctor Robotic,
is turning people into mind slaves.
Now YOU must put a stop to his
plans before it's too late!

978 1 4451 3958 6 pb
978 1 4451 3961 6 eBook

You are a young wizard.
The evil Witch Queen has captured
Prince Bron. Now YOU must rescue
him before she takes control of
Nine Mountain kingdom!